¹/93

CARTONS,

CANS,

AND ORANGE PEELS

CARTONS,

CANS,

AND ORANGE PEELS

WHERE DOES YOUR GARBAGE GO?

BY

JOANNA FOSTER

CLARION BOOKS
NEW YORK

For Joe and Gigi

Clarion Books

a Houghton Mifflin Company imprint

215 Park Avenue South, New York, NY 10003

Library of Congress Cataloging-in-Publication Data
Foster, Joanna.
 Cartons, cans, and orange peels — where does your garbage go? / by Joanna
Foster.
  p. cm.
 Includes bibliographical references.
 Summary: Outlines the composition of garbage and trash and discusses the
various methods of disposing of it with an emphasis on recycling.
 ISBN 0-395-56436-0
 1. Refuse and refuse disposal — Juvenile literature. 2. Recycling (Waste,
etc.) — Juvenile literature. [1. Refuse and refuse disposal. 2. Recycling
(Waste)] I. Title.
TD792.F67
628.4′4 — dc20   90-2616
                    CIP
                 AC

Book design by Janis Owens
Frontispiece photograph by Joanna Foster

Printed on recycled paper

WOZ 10 9 8 7 6 5 4 3 2 1

CONTENTS

1. IN AND OUT OF THE GARBAGE CAN / 7

2. THE TOWN DUMP / 10

3. BURY IT IN A LANDFILL / 12

4. GARBAGE EATERS / 16

5. CHANGE INTO EARTH / 19

6. BURN IT AND MAKE ENERGY / 22

7. REUSE AND RECYCLE—TRASH THAT ESCAPES / 27

8. SEPARATE TO RECYCLE / 35

9. PACKAGING AND PAPER—QUICKLY THROWN AWAY / 44

10. HAZARDOUS WASTE IN A GARBAGE CAN / 50

11. THINK ABOUT GARBAGE / 55

GLOSSARY / 58

SOME SOURCES FOR MORE INFORMATION / 60

ACKNOWLEDGMENTS / 62

INDEX / 63

If you divide what is discarded by weight,

40.2% is paper;
7% glass;
8.6% metal;
8.1% plastics;
8.3% rubber, leather, cloth, and wood;
6.8% food waste;
17.7% yard waste;
3.2% miscellaneous.

(Foster)

CHAPTER ONE

IN AND OUT OF
THE GARBAGE CAN

It is the middle of the night. There is a clattering sound and then, *Crash!* One of the garbage cans has been tipped over. A big dog is eagerly pawing through cans, paper, bones, orange peels, and other garbage.

What bad luck for somebody! All that garbage will have to be picked up in the morning. It needs to be back in the can before the garbage truck comes. The two cans are always full the night before collection day. In fact, this can was so full that the lid wouldn't fit on it.

Garbage is a mess to pick up! First there is the food: orange peels, bones, leftover mashed potatoes, coffee grounds and eggshells, half a sandwich, and a tangle of cold spaghetti. Most of this is wet and soggy.

Then there are the bottles and cans. They have rolled all over the place. There is an empty applesauce jar, a shampoo bottle, tuna fish cans, a can that once held insect spray, soda bottles, and beer cans.

There is plenty of plastic too: soft plastic bags from the grocery store and the dry cleaner's, a molded plastic box that once held a midget racing car, a large milk container, broken plastic coffee cups, and the cheeseburger boxes from the fast food store down the street.

And there is paper everywhere: newspaper, envelopes and advertisements, soggy paper towels, crumpled napkins, a cereal box, frozen food and juice containers.

In with all this is a bag of used diapers, an old pair of boots, a torn sheet, four dead batteries, and a half-used can of paint. Whoever has to pick up this mess usually wonders how one family can make so much garbage!

This family is no different from most others in the United States. Today, most Americans are tossing out about thirteen hundred pounds of garbage a year. That's over three and a half pounds per person, every day. Almost half of this is paper and cardboard, another fifth is glass or metal. No one sees their thirteen hundred pounds of garbage all at once, because every few days it is taken away.

Early in the morning a large collection truck comes by. Workers jump off the truck, lift up the heavy garbage cans, and empty them into an open place at the back of the truck. A blade comes down and with a great crunching sound pushes the garbage inside. The garbage is pressed toward the front of the truck into as small a space as possible. Seven

Collecting solid waste costs billions of dollars a year.

([*Greenville, SC*] *Waste Age*, National Solid Waste Management Association)

tons of garbage will be squashed into the truck before the morning is over.

In front of one building, someone has put out an old baby carriage, a sofa with a missing leg, and an old refrigerator. Big things like this are called bulky waste and are usually picked up separately. A special name for large metal trash such as refrigerators, bathtubs, and stoves is *white goods.*

In many towns the sign on the side of the collection truck may say Refuse Removal. In cities, it often says Sanitation Department. Though the collectors are correctly called sanitation workers, many people still say "garbage men." In fact most of us call everything we throw away "garbage." The true meaning of the word *garbage* is waste food, such as an orange peel or half a sandwich. Everything else, everything that is not food, is correctly called refuse or *trash.* The combination of garbage and trash is called *solid waste.* Though food can be mushy and there can be liquids mixed in with some of the trash, most of it is solid enough to pick up. Waste that is liquid, like sour milk or soapy water, is usually poured down the drain. It becomes part of the sewage that with the waste water goes into a septic tank or flows away in the sewer pipes to the sewage disposal facility.

A lot of solid waste is household waste, collected from people's garbage cans. Still more is collected from schools, offices, small factories, and stores.

In some towns and cities, solid waste is collected by private companies. In others, the city collects it. Billions of dollars are spent to collect and dispose of solid waste. Often, only one thing costs taxpayers more, and that is keeping the schools open.

Every day, all over the country, thousands of trucks are collecting solid waste. But that is only the beginning. All these thousands of trucks packed tight with garbage and trash have to go somewhere to dump what they've collected.

CHAPTER TWO

THE TOWN DUMP

It used to be that all collection trucks headed for the town dump. They would drive into the dump, back up, and, with a roar, empty their loads near the garbage already there.

This great mound of solid waste was ugly. And how it smelled! Rats, flies, and sea gulls loved it. The town dump was an easy place to find plenty to eat. Unfortunately, rats and flies in such numbers can spread disease and be dangerous to people's health.

There were often fires at a dump. Some of the fires were lit on purpose to make the mound smaller or to discourage the rats and flies. For many years, these fires

Towns no longer use open garbage dumps like this one.

(Rhode Island Department of Environmental Management, Division of Environmental Coordination)

didn't bother people, except when the wind blew over the dump and brought the sharp-smelling smoke in their direction. Now people know that the smoke from slowly burning waste not only smells bad, but also pollutes the fresh air with gases and tiny pieces of ash that make people's eyes sting and can hurt their lungs.

Rain, of course, fell on the dump. For a long time, no one thought this was a problem. Then some towns found that germs and toxic chemicals were poisoning their rivers and drinking water. Scientists found that many of the poisons were coming from the town dump. Every time it rained, the rainwater soaked down through the mound of garbage and trash. As the rainwater seeped down, it picked up germs and chemicals from the solid waste. When the water reached the bottom and escaped into the river, it carried the germs and chemicals with it. Water that has been polluted like this is called *leachate*.

Today there are few open dumps. Instead of simply dumping their garbage and trash, most towns now bury it.

More than 450,000 tons of garbage and trash are collected each day and must go somewhere.

(Rhode Island Solid Waste Management Corporation)

CHAPTER THREE

BURY IT IN A LANDFILL

Landfills, like this one in California, are regularly checked by official inspectors to be sure they are operating properly and following regulations.

([Dulce Ledo] Monterey Regional Waste Management District)

When solid waste is buried, people don't have to look at it. Rats and flies are discouraged from living in it. There is less chance of fires.

What kind of a place is picked to bury waste? Usually, a town looks for a low area that can be filled. Sometimes it is a quarry, sometimes a valley. Since the solid waste will be used to fill in the land, this site is called a *landfill*.

In some cases, after the hole itself has been filled, a town will keep adding layer after layer of solid waste. Many landfills actually become mountains of garbage and trash. Several of these new mountains have been nicknamed Mount Trashmore.

Here is what happens each day at a landfill. The full collection trucks begin to arrive about ten o'clock. Off to one side, several bulldozers and earthmovers are waiting for them. Each truck backs up to unload. The driver pushes a lever and the heavy body of the truck raises up. With a crashing thud a mass of crushed food, paper, cans, rags, and other trash falls to the ground.

After the first few loads, the bulldozer driver goes to work. He drives over the mounds of garbage and trash, back and forth, crushing and flattening them as much as possible. Skill and care are needed to drive across these uneven shifting mounds and not tip over.

Piles of earth stand to the side of the area where the bulldozers are working. When the solid waste has been flattened as much as possible, the drivers begin to bulldoze earth over it. By evening, there will be at least six inches of earth over every bit of the waste brought in that day. No flying papers or rusting cans are left to be seen. Nothing but earth is visible until the next morning, when the collection trucks begin arriving to add another layer to the landfill.

About 73% of our solid waste is being buried in landfills.

(Waste Age, NSWMA)

To prepare a new landfill site, the bottom and sides are lined with several materials. This is a heavy plastic liner.

(*[Live Oaks Landfill, Georgia] Waste Age*, NSWMA)

Solid waste buried under layers of earth is called a *sanitary landfill*. It is called sanitary because it seems to be a clean way of getting rid of garbage and trash. There is no smoke to pollute the air, and water pollution can usually be controlled, if the landfill is not too close to a river or a source of drinking water.

Landfills that have been opened since 1980 have been designed to be as safe as possible. A new landfill is lined with layers of clay, gravel, and heavy plastic so the leachate won't leak out. Pipes are put in to bring out the gases and the leachate, which is then cleaned.

Eventually a landfill can't hold any more. The hole is full and the garbage mountain is as high as it can be built. The landfill must be closed. The town must find a new place to put the tons of solid waste the collection trucks are picking up every morning.

There are still marshes and swamps that no one seems to be using. Is it possible that these could become new landfills? Scientists tell us that birds and fish need the marshes and swamps to live in. Such places are important in controlling floods, and they also absorb dirt and some toxic chemicals from the water, keeping these from polluting rivers and lakes. Don't fill them up, say the scientists. Put the garbage somewhere else.

Most people don't want a landfill near their homes. They consider it ugly and smelly. The trucks that go in and out of a landfill are noisy and so heavy they shake houses as they go by. So, many towns and cities have run out of good places for landfills. There is no place to bury solid waste nearby, so they must send it miles away. In this case, the town's collection trucks take their loads to a transfer station where the garbage and trash are dumped into a much larger cross-country trailer truck. This truck may travel two or three days to get to a landfill. Some cities send their solid waste so far away that it isn't even buried in the same state. The farther the trucks have to go, the more money it costs.

When a landfill is full, a cap of clay and a final layer of earth, six feet deep, are put over the solid waste. Grass and bushes are planted, and it often is made into a park. Walk in one of these parks, and it will seem as though you are walking on solid ground. But the ground is not as solid as you think. It is not solid enough to build a house on, and will not be for many years.

Under the top layer of earth, the great mass of solid waste is changing. As it changes it is slowly sinking and settling. In this landfill, rats and flies may not be feeding on your garbage, but billions of other, much smaller creatures are.

This is a landfill that has been closed and capped and is now part of a park.

(Waste Age, NSWMA)

CHAPTER FOUR

GARBAGE EATERS

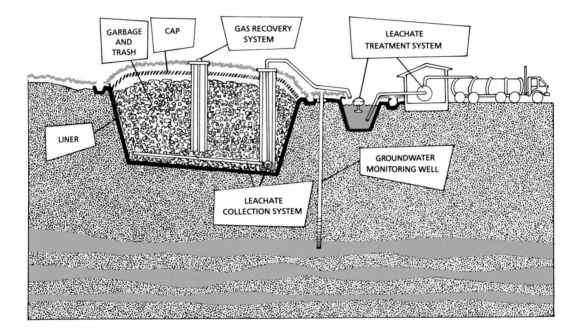

Inside a landfill, there are millions of tiny living things called *microorganisms* or microbes. They are feasting on the mashed potatoes, orange peels, stale bread, and tons of other scraps people have thrown away. How these microbes can eat! Every few seconds, each one eats its weight in food.

Some of these microbes are fungi and some are bacteria. You may have seen the fungi on moldy bread. Fungi start eating and growing even before food reaches a landfill. Other microorganisms, like various kinds of bacteria, are too small to see without a microscope. Even though we can't

Diagram of a landfill.

(Adapted from a National Solid Waste Management Association diagram.)

16

see these microorganisms, they play an important part in the cycle of life on earth.

As microbes feed on the garbage, they change it. Food no longer looks or feels or smells as it once did. Old cabbage leaves, squashed tomatoes, and banana peels all crumble into tiny particles or turn to gas. This changing process is called *decomposition*. If you say something is rotting or decaying, it is decomposing.

Decomposing garbage smells terrible. That is because of gases which the microbes create as they eat. One of these gases is ammonia. You can smell ammonia around wet trampled-down grass or fresh manure.

Another kind of gas created by bacteria has no smell at all but is very powerful. It is called *methane*. Methane gas catches fire quickly, and if trapped may explode. Though dangerous in a landfill, methane is a useful gas if controlled. It can be used to heat houses, cook food, and even run engines. Many landfills now have pipes running down into them to catch the gases being created and put the methane

Bacteria like these are so small that about 250,000 could fit into the period at the end of this sentence.

(Cornell University)

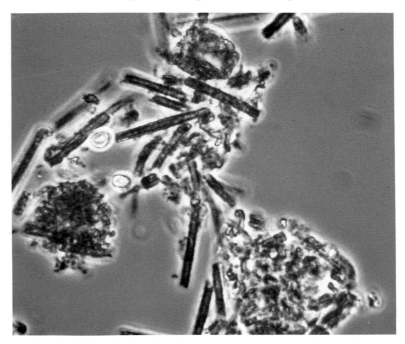

to use. For example, the Settler's Hill landfill in Geneva, Illinois, regularly supplies fuel to 7,500 homes.

In addition to food, microbes will feed on crumpled paper napkins, dead flowers, a cotton sheet, leather shoes, leaves, and fur mittens. Anything that microorganisms will eat is called *biodegradable*. The words *decay, decompose,* and *degradable* all mean that a thing breaks apart and changes into something else. Add *bio* to the word *degradable,* and it means that living microorganisms can make the change. Things that are biodegradable most often were made from something that was once alive, such as a plant or an animal. A paper napkin was once wood pulp made from a tree. Leather shoes were made from the skin of an animal. Microorganisms cannot feed on metal, glass, ceramic, or plastics. Therefore, bottles, cans, dishes, and other objects made from these materials are not biodegradable.

In a landfill, decomposition takes a long time. Some bacteria need air to live and eat. After a few years there is very little air inside the landfill, and these important bacteria die. Only the kind of bacteria that can live without air keeps working, but very slowly. Packed in its airless tomb, much of the solid waste stops decomposing.

CHAPTER FIVE

CHANGE INTO EARTH

Grass clippings, leaves, twigs, tree trunks, weeds, and other yard waste are also buried in landfills. Even a small town will have an enormous amount of yard waste each year. All the leaves that are raked up in the fall, the branches and trees that are blown down in a bad storm, all the Christmas trees that are discarded each January can take up as much as one fifth of the space in a city's landfill.

Long ago, farmers found that if they piled up all their old straw, leaves, stalks, and manure, microorganisms would change the smelly pile into a mound of good-smelling black earth in about a year. Mixed into the soil, this black earth gave new plants nitrogen which they needed to grow, and helped keep water near their roots.

The black earth made from decomposed plants is called humus or *compost*. Many gardeners stack leaves, grass clippings, dead flower stalks, and weeds to make compost. Some put apple cores, carrot peelings, and other leftover fruits and vegetables into their compost piles. They may add horse or cow manure. Some even add shredded newspaper, knowing that the microorganisms will eat that up too. If compost is mixed up every so often and kept moist, it will have the right amount of water and air for bacteria to multiply. Then leaves and garbage can become compost in a few months.

Compost is so good for gardens that people often go to the store to buy it. But for years homeowners have put tons of leaves out with their trash, and towns have buried this

Leaves, grass, and other yard waste can be turned into compost.

(Foster; International Process Systems)

yard waste in their landfills. In the early 1980s, a few towns started composting leaves to save space in their landfills. Now more are doing it. The leaves are piled in long rows in a large field, kept moist, and turned over every so often to give the bacteria the air they need. Some towns are also chipping up discarded Christmas trees and giving people the chips to use as protective mulch around trees and bushes.

The possibility of composting not only yard waste but all biodegradable waste is being explored. This would include even the sludge that remains when liquid waste, or sewage, has been cleaned. Composting of yard waste and sludge is often done in a large building. If you were to visit this composting facility, you would see practically nobody there. "But there are millions of workers here," the supervisor will tell you. "We do everything we can to make it easy for our earthmakers. We grind up what they eat. We are always checking that they have enough air and water. So, our workers never quit. They work day and night and can make compost in twenty-one days." These amazing earthmakers are of course millions of microorganisms, changing biodegradable waste into useful earth.

Leaves are collected and put in long rows. These are being turned over to ensure that the bacteria have enough air.

(Waste Age, NSWMA)

In this building, shredded leaves and branches are combined with sewage sludge and loaded at the front of the trough. The machine turns and slowly moves the mixture along to the other end where it comes out as compost.

(International Process Systems)

CHAPTER SIX

BURN IT AND MAKE ENERGY

In a modern incinerator the fire is kept above 2,000 degrees Fahrenheit.

(Ogden Martin Systems Inc.)

A hundred years ago, many cities decided that instead of sending their solid waste straight to a dump, they would burn it first. Ashes and cinders took up much less space and harmful germs were destroyed. To burn the waste they built large furnaces or *incinerators*.

For a while this seemed a good way to get rid of garbage and trash. But in the last fifty years our air has become hazy with smoke and gases. Scientists found that cars, factories, and incinerators were causing most of this air pollution. Many of the incinerators were old and not working well. Cities turned back to burying their garbage and the old incinerators were torn down. Landfills filled up much faster, and now many have closed. Each year we create more and more garbage, but each year there are fewer and fewer landfills in which to put it.

Burning solid waste is still a way to use the space in landfills more efficiently. But if the waste is burned, it must be in an incinerator that catches the smoke and any toxic gases before they get out and pollute the air. In new incinerators the fire is very hot, much hotter than in open dumps or in the older incinerators. The hotter the fire, the more things will burn. Glass and dishes made of ceramic don't actually burn, but if the fire is very hot, they melt and crumble. For every ten truckloads of garbage and trash that are fed into the incinerator, only one truckload of ash and cinders remains.

Much of the solid waste is turned into heat. In the old incinerators this heat would have gone up the smokestack, but now it is caught and used. The energy in that heat is changed into electrical energy, or electricity, that is supplied to homes nearby. The garbage you throw away one day could return in a few days as the electricity you use to turn on your television set. This new kind of incinerator is called a *waste-to-energy facility*. It is also called a *resource recovery*

The waste-to-energy facility in Bristol, Connecticut. In 1991 there were 150 such facilities in the United States.

(Ogden Martin Systems Inc.)

facility because it recovers — makes use of — the heat energy in solid waste.

A waste-to-energy facility is a huge building with at least one tall chimney. There are only a few windows, but there is a gigantic doorway. Each collection truck with its full load of garbage and trash drives through the doorway and stops. When the driver is given the signal, he pushes a lever and empties his whole load onto the floor.

An inspector with sharp eyes checks this mound of solid waste for such things as drums of chemicals, car batteries, old air conditioners, and asbestos that could injure the workers in the facility or cause air pollution. These will not go into the furnace. The rest of the load is pushed over and into the storage pit.

This great scoop steadily feeds two-ton loads into the incinerator, day and night. About 15% of solid waste in the United States is incinerated.

(Ogden Martin Systems Inc.)

More than two thousand tons of all kinds of garbage and trash are in this huge storage pit. A giant scoop moves back and forth over the pit. Every few minutes the operator lowers the scoop and grabs two or three tons of solid waste. He moves it over to a chute and drops it in. Slowly the garbage and trash move down into a very hot fire.

Day and night, without stop, ton after ton of solid waste is fed into the fire, which burns inside a specially designed furnace. Water runs through rows of pipes on all sides of the furnace. The water picks up so much heat from the fire that it expands into powerful steam. More pipes take the steam to another part of the facility where it is used to keep an electric generator spinning.

The parts of the solid waste that don't burn drop to the bottom of the furnace as ash and cinders. Another part flies up from the flames. Heat changes some of the solid waste into gases and tiny pieces of soot. Since it floats above the flames, this soot is called *fly ash*.

Most of the gases are commonly found in our air. But a small portion is a mixture of acidic gases and chemicals like chlorine, which can become a gaseous form of hydrochloric acid. This mixture could pollute the air.

Before the gases go up the chimney, they are sent through pollution control devices to be cleaned. One device is called a *scrubber*. When an acidic gas like hydrochloric acid goes through the scrubber, it is sprayed with an antacid that combines with the acid and neutralizes it, making it harmless. The antacid in the scrubber works in much the same way as the antacid tablets people take to relieve indigestion.

The fly ash is also trapped to keep it from escaping up the chimney. One device, called a *baghouse*, sucks the ash out of the air like a vacuum cleaner. The fly ash will be sent to a landfill where it will be buried very carefully. Fly ash still contains some of the toxic chemicals that came from the garbage.

The bottom ash that drops out of the furnace is cooled and then moved along a conveyor belt. It too will go to a landfill and be buried. Before it is loaded onto a truck, however, it is picked over by a giant magnet which attracts anything made of iron or steel. As the black ash goes under the magnet, an iron rod, old bed springs, and a couple of sooty cans rise out of the ash. They stick to the magnet, which takes them to one side. The iron and steel rescued from the ash will be sent to a steel mill and used to make new steel.

Burning this garbage reduces it to a much smaller amount of ash (insert).

(Ogden Martin Systems Inc.)

CHAPTER SEVEN

REUSE AND RECYCLE –
TRASH THAT ESCAPES

These masks started as plastic milk containers to which the artists added such things as ice cream sticks, paper towel tubes, ribbon spools, part of a wooden lamp, and a plastic coat hook (the mouth on the blue and pink mask).

(Carol Young)

Not all trash ends up in a garbage can. Some escapes by being reused or recycled. Most of us would throw out a torn dress, a worn-out tire, or a broken chair leg. But some people keep throwaways like these and transform them in marvelous ways.

Beautiful quilts can be made out of worn-out clothes. Since colonial times, people have cut old clothes into patches and sewn them together into bed quilts. Nowadays scraps of cloth and leather are also used to make patchwork pillows, purses, or even vests and skirts.

You may have seen old tires used as playground swings or boat bumpers on the side of a dock. In Taos, New Mexico, Michael Reynolds uses old tires to build houses. The tires, filled with dirt, make the outside walls, and the inside walls are made of aluminum cans! These are then covered with plaster or adobe to make them smooth.

"Wood picked up on the street can be gold." That's what the artist Louise Nevelson said. For years she collected wooden crates, broken chair legs, baseball bats, rolling pins, and all the crazy scraps of wood she could find. Putting them together in imaginative ways, she created exciting sculpture that is now in museums all over the world for people to enjoy. Louise Nevelson is just one of many artists who have turned trash into handsome works of art.

Often toys, clothes, books, and even furniture are discarded before they are worn out. They are still good, but the owner doesn't want them anymore. These can be given to a resale shop or put into a garage sale — sometimes called a tag sale, yard sale, or rummage sale. Instead of becoming trash, they will be used and enjoyed by someone else.

Some recycling symbols. The triangle of arrows means the product can be recycled. To show that boxes and other paper products are made out of recycled paper, the triangle is used in a circle.

(American Paper Institute, Steel Can Recycling Institute)

A factory can sometimes save money by using what another factory must throw away. Nutshells are an example. When walnuts are canned, there is always a great pile of walnut shells to throw away. Someone looked at these hard, sharp shells and had an idea. Now those discarded shells are used to make a cleaner for the bottom of ships. Reusing trash like this gives it a longer life and saves it from being wasted.

Trash can have many "lives" when it is recycled. Recycling means that an item goes in a circle from factory to customer and then back to the factory where material in it is made into something new. Some materials can be recycled again and again. An aluminum soda can is a good example.

Fireplace tools that one household no longer needed are a bargain quickly snapped up at this family tag sale.

(Foster)

Most of the aluminum we use every day is lightweight and has a shiny gray color. Aluminum doesn't look that way when it comes out of the ground, because it is trapped in chunks of red bauxite rock. The red rock goes to a refinery, where the aluminum is extracted using water, chemicals, and a lot of electricity. While the aluminum is hot and very soft, it is molded into blocks, or *ingots*. These are shipped to can factories where they are squeezed into thin, flat sheets from which the cans are made. The cans are filled with soda and are ready to be sold.

Refining aluminum from this bauxite ore takes twenty times more electricity than recycling the aluminum in these bales of cans (opposite page).

(Reynolds Metals Co.)

CHAPTER EIGHT

SEPARATE TO RECYCLE

This boy disposes of the family's empty aluminum cans while his father takes glass bottles to another bin. This is one of thousands of recycling centers around the country.

(Foster)

Cans in one box, plastic bottles in another, glass bottles and jars in a third, and old newspapers in a brown paper bag: many people in the United States no longer throw everything into the garbage pail. They keep separate the things that can be recycled.

Separate and sort. That is where recycling begins. In thousands of communities, people take their cans, bottles, and paper to the local recycling center. Most of these recycling centers have opened up since the late 1960s. Some materials like rags, scrap metal, and newspapers were being collected and reused long before that, but in the 1960s environmentalists began making people aware of the need to care for the earth and conserve its resources.

In many towns, a special collection truck picks up materials to be recycled. The collector puts bottles and cans into one part of the truck and newspapers into the other. When the recycling truck is full, it heads for the MRF. MRF, pronounced "Murf," is the abbreviation for *materials recycling facility*. At the MRF, more sorting and separating take place, and the newspapers, plastic, glass, aluminum cans, and steel cans are shipped out to different factories.

The driver brings the recycling truck into the MRF, backs up to a mountain of bottles and cans, and dumps that part of his load. He then dumps his newspapers in a different pile.

The pile of newspapers is steadily pushed onto a conveyor belt that takes it to a baler. Here the newspapers are squeezed together into a large, heavy block, called a *bale*. The bales are fastened with metal or plastic strips so they

Santa Rosa, California, is one of the towns where special trucks pick up bottles, cans, and newspapers for recycling.

(Waste Age, NSWMA)

won't come apart when they are taken by truck to the paper mill.

Two people watch the newspaper as it heads toward the baler. These are the pickers. They pick out any plastic bags or magazines that have gotten in with the newspapers by mistake. Magazines are made of a different kind of paper, which has a thin clay coating on it, giving it a smooth glossy surface. Many also have a tough glue in the binding. The clay and the glue are hard to separate from the paper, making magazines more difficult and more costly to recycle.

Unloading some of the 140 tons of newspaper, cans, and bottles the MRF in Johnston, Rhode Island, sorts each day.

(Ryerson Van Deusen)

The bottles and cans also start their journey through the MRF by being pushed onto a conveyor belt. Moving along the belt are brown, green, and clear glass bottles, aluminum cans, plastic bottles, and steel cans. All of these are mixed up together, along with pieces of broken glass and odd things thrown in by mistake, such as a toy fire truck, a broken plate, a flashlight, or a plastic football helmet.

Metal, plastic, and glass cans and bottles are going under the magnet that will separate out the steel cans.

(Rhode Island Solid Waste Management Corporation)

How to get this all sorted out? People do some of the sorting. These pickers' hands move fast, flying back and forth, as they pull out the unwanted items.

The rest goes on into the machines that, with much noisy shaking, clinking, rumbling, and banging, separate the metal, glass, and plastic. Sorting machines are designed to separate the material by its weight, size, color, or some other characteristic.

The steel cans are different because they are made of a ferrous metal, containing iron. Ferrous metal will stick to a magnet. As the trash goes along the conveyor belt, a strong magnet lifts all the steel cans up and out to a separate box.

Weight is an important difference between the glass, plastic, and aluminum that remain. Glass bottles are the heaviest. Some machines use a strong blast of air to blow the light plastic and aluminum off the conveyor belt. Another machine sends everything down a slope against a curtain of metal strings. The glass is heavy enough to push right through the curtain and reach the bottom. The lighter aluminum and plastic stay behind and move off in another direction.

The aluminum and plastic are separated using another magnet. This is not a ferrous magnet which attracts steel. It is an eddy current magnet, and it works in just the opposite way on the aluminum cans — instead of picking them up, it pushes them away. The eddy current magnet acts like an invisible hand, tossing the aluminum cans off the conveyor belt against a backboard from which they rebound into a box.

Glass needs to be separated by color, and this is done by hand. The brown amber glass goes in one box, the green emerald glass goes in another, and the clear flint glass goes into a third box. Little pieces of broken glass are hard to separate by color. These are sifted out as the bottles go over a screen that shakes back and forth. Pieces of ceramic cups

Glass is made out of sand (two piles on the left), limestone, and soda ash (right rear). The pieces of recycled green bottles (center) will be mixed and melted with more of these ingredients to make a new batch of green glass, which, in turn, will be shaped into bottles.

(Glass Packaging Institute)

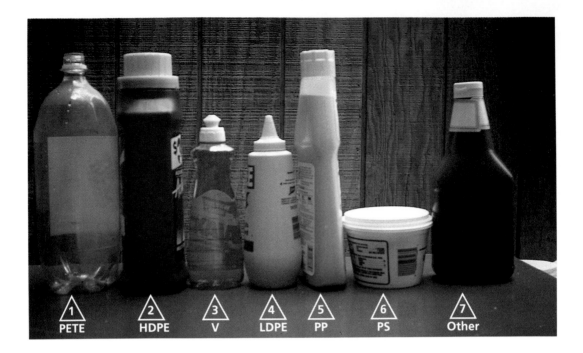

| 1 PETE | 2 HDPE | 3 V | 4 LDPE | 5 PP | 6 PS | 7 Other |

and plates must be carefully picked or sifted out. Clean glass can be recycled over and over again. But if small pieces of ceramic get trapped in the glass as it is melted at the factory, the new glass is ruined and can't be used.

The plastic bottles will also be sorted by pickers. The most common plastic containers to be recycled are soda bottles and large milk or water bottles. Though these look as if they are made of the same thing, they're not. At least forty-five different kinds of plastics exist and each is made of something different.

Six kinds of plastics are commonly used for bottles and other containers. To help people tell them apart, many of them bear a code of a number in a triangle. This is the code:

PETE (or PET) — polyethylene terephthalate, used for such things as soda bottles and peanut butter jars.

HDPE — high density polyethylene, used for large milk and water bottles and the base on some soda bottles.

Each number, 1 through 6, stands for a different plastic. Number 7 is made of layers of different plastics. Look for the code (shown below each) on the bottom of a container.

(Foster; Society of Plastics Industry)

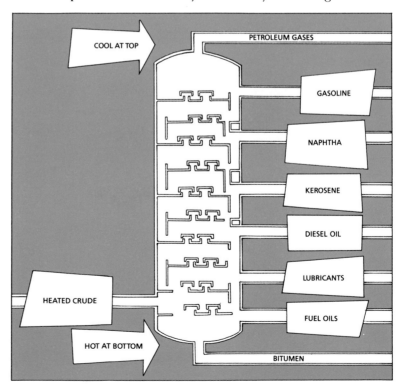

3 V (or PVC) — polyvinyl chloride, used for cooking oil containers and film for wrapping meat.

4 LDPE — low-density polyethylene, used for bags.

5 PP — polypropylene, used for many snack food wrappers.

6 PS — polystyrene, used in foam products and such things as cottage cheese containers and cookie package trays.

7 Other plastic, or containers made from a combination of plastics.

Almost all plastics are made from *crude oil*. This is the name for oil as it is pumped from the ground. At a refinery, crude oil is separated into various gases and liquids. The liquids include the motor oil used in cars and the heating oil used in houses. Some of the gases are used to make plastics.

In the names of some of the different plastics, you will see the letters *poly*. *Poly* means "many," and it is a clue to the fact that plastics are made by chemically fastening or chain-

When crude oil is heated to boiling, it separates into various parts. Naphtha is a combination of light gases. One of these is ethylene, which is used to make polyethylene.

COOL AT TOP

PETROLEUM GASES

GASOLINE

NAPHTHA

KEROSENE

DIESEL OIL

LUBRICANTS

HEATED CRUDE

FUEL OILS

HOT AT BOTTOM

BITUMEN

ing many, many molecules of a gas together. When the molecules are linked in this way, they form a material that can be pressed into solid pellets.

To make a large soda bottle, pellets of PET are heated until they become a thick soup. This is squirted into a mold. When it cools, the neck of the bottle is the right size, but the body of the bottle is only a long narrow tube. Next the body is heated until it is soft and rubbery. Air is blown into it, forcing the plastic to expand and assume the shape of the mold, its final shape. The PET cools and hardens into a finished soda bottle.

PET bottles are easy to recycle. The old bottles are chipped, cleaned, and then heated. Once again the plastic melts into a thick soup. But recycled PET and other plastics are generally not used to make food or drink containers again. Recycled PET is often made into fibers which are then woven into carpets or used as filling for winter jackets. Recycled milk bottles, made of the plastic HDPE, are used to make such things as park benches, flowerpots, and fence posts. More kinds of plastics will be recycled as uses for them are developed.

Plastics can take any form: a thread, a bottle, a thin sheet, a firm table. Because of their versatility, they have been used for more and more of the things that once were made of wood, paper, metal, glass, or ceramic. Plastics are lighter in weight than most other materials and they often cost less to produce. Plastic forks and spoons, for instance, are so cheap that people think nothing of using them once and throwing them away. Silver forks and spoons, on the other hand, are used for years and sometimes passed down from generation to generation.

There are drawbacks, however. Because of their chemical structure, plastics are not biodegradable. Some may become brittle and crack, but no plastic will rot or rust. This is an advantage if you are building a fence or a boat dock. It

Chips from recycled plastic soda bottles can be melted and made into fibers such as those in this fiber-filled jacket.

(Plastics Recycling Foundation; Council for Solid Waste Solutions)

is a disadvantage when plastic bags, bottles, foam cups, and fishline are carelessly littered. The dangerous gases used to make some plastics may escape if they are carelessly burned. Though plastics are lightweight, their bulk makes up about a fifth of our household waste.

CHAPTER NINE

PACKAGING AND PAPER – QUICKLY THROWN AWAY

Think how many things are made for us to use only once and then throw away: candy bar wrappers, plastic bags, paper plates, soda cans, foam cups, aluminum take-out dishes, paper towels, razors for shaving, diapers for babies. Newspapers by the millions are bought, read, and thrown out every day. These disposable things make life easier in many ways. They don't cost a lot of money, they save time, and they don't have to be washed and dried or taken care of.

Of course, once they are used and tossed out, all these disposable things become tons and tons of trash. After one use, they are buried, burned, or recycled. We now use so many quick throwaways that they make up more than half of what goes into our garbage cans.

Like the candy bar paper and the soda can, many of these quick throwaways are wrappers or containers. They are the packaging for food, clothing, toys — almost everything we buy. Look into a shopping cart as it pulls up to the checkout counter. There are green grapes in a thin plastic bag, milk in a carton, cereal in a box, hamburger on a plastic tray sealed in clear plastic, salad dressing in a glass bottle, and individual boxes of juice. All these will be carried home in at least one more package, a plastic or brown paper grocery bag.

Sometimes there is a package within a package. Inside

How much of this cart full of groceries is packaging? Look to the right. Once the products were used, this much packaging got thrown out.

(Foster)

the cardboard cereal box, for instance, there is another thin package to help keep the cereal fresh. Some packaging is made of a combination of materials. The individual juice boxes are made of a layer of plastic, a layer of paperboard, and a layer of aluminum foil permanently stuck together. After the boxes are filled, they are put in another package of plastic shrink-wrap. The paper, plastic, and aluminum can't be separated, so these juice boxes can't be recycled. More than four billion of them are tossed in the trash every year.

Have we gotten in the habit of using more quick throwaways than we really need? Is there packaging that isn't necessary? Some people think so. They look for ways to reduce the amount of packaging they bring home. They carry home their groceries in cloth or string bags which can be used again and again. They buy one large container of food or drinks rather than many individual ones. A few companies are also trying to redesign their packaging so that it uses less material or can be recycled.

More than a third of all our solid waste is paper. Egg cartons, notebook paper, newspapers, books, magazines, computer paper, cardboard, corrugated shipping boxes, paper cups and plates, and paper bags are only a few of the paper products we use.

Many people now shop by mail or telephone. To reach them, more and more catalogs and advertisements are sent in the mail. Some of these are welcome, but many are not wanted or needed, and get quickly junked.

Paper is biodegradable. Microbes will eat shredded paper in a compost pile. In most landfills, however, there is not enough air and therefore not enough microbes to degrade it. Paper burns well in an incinerator and many kinds can be recycled.

Newspapers, cardboard cartons, writing paper, and computer paper can all be used to make new paper or cardboard. Like metals, glass, and plastics, paper needs to

Bales of newspaper ready to be shipped to the paper mill.

(Rhode Island Department of Environmental Management, Division of Environmental Coordination)

be separated to be recycled. It can't have metal or plastic, like the thin aluminum lining in a food container or the plastic window in a business envelope, attached to it. If there is leftover tomato sauce, bacon fat, or paint on the paper, it is hard to recycle. Paper waste is also best recycled if different kinds of paper aren't mixed together.

It takes about seventeen trees to make one ton of paper, and millions of tons of paper are used every year. The mills that recycle paper are different from those that originally make the paper from wood. Not all of these mills are in the United States. Americans have so much newspaper to recycle that boatloads of it are shipped to countries like Japan, Mexico, and South Korea. There it is often made into cardboard for boxes in which cameras, television sets, and sweaters are shipped back to the United States.

At the paper recycling mill, the old paper is dumped into a huge machine, the pulper pit, where it is mixed with water and heated. Paper is made of tiny wood fibers, crisscrossed every which way and sticking tightly together. When the paper gets wet and warm, these fibers come apart. Eventually it turns into a thick mushy pulp.

There may be stray paper clips, staples, or crumbs of dirt in with the paper. To get these out, the pulp is forced through screens and then spun around in large tanks. The stray material will either be caught by the screens or fall to the bottom of the tanks.

After another washing the pulp is spread out on screens to dry. The water is pressed out of the pulp, and the wood fibers begin to knit together again. Heavy rollers press them even more tightly together until they form one very long, wide, flat sheet. If the sheet is cardboard made from old newspapers, it is usually gray, because the black ink that was on the newspaper has mixed with the white paper. You will see this gray color on the inside of boxes made from recycled newspaper.

Recycled paper can also be white. In fact, often you cannot see the difference between recycled paper and paper that is made from wood pulp. To make the paper white,

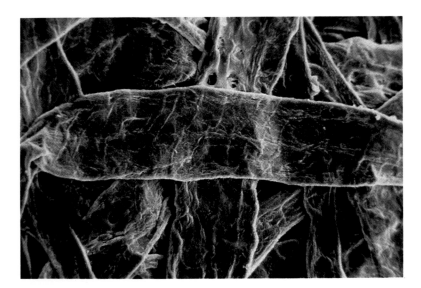

Paper seen under a microscope shows the interwoven wood fibers from which it is made.

(P. H. Glatfelter Company)

48

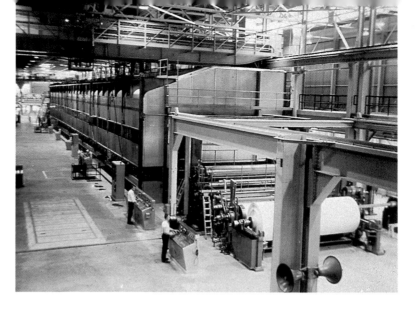

This machine makes a mile of paper every three minutes.

(P. H. Glatfelter Company)

chemicals are used to take the ink out of the pulp and to bleach it.

Some companies advertise that they use recycled paper. They put "100% recycled paper" or "Made with recycled fibers" at the bottom of a letter or on a box. Often paper is made of a combination of fresh wood pulp and recycled paper pulp, because in each recycling some of the wood fibers break and get shorter, tending to make the paper softer and weaker.

In the 1980s a lot of paper was collected for recycling, but there were not enough special paper mills to handle all of it. Many people were discouraged and stopped saving paper. The paper mills that do recycling are very expensive to build. Many more customers buying recycled paper are needed to create the demand that encourages building new mills. A few states have promoted recycling by passing a law that publishers must use some recycled paper in all newspapers.

Recycling is an important way to cut down on waste because it saves not only trees, metal, and other natural resources but also energy. Reducing the number of quick throwaways we use is another way to cut down the amount of solid waste that must be burned or buried every day.

CHAPTER TEN

HAZARDOUS WASTE IN A GARBAGE CAN

Batteries, house paint, floor polish, drain cleaner, insect spray, and motor oil are dangerous items to throw in the garbage can. They are all *hazardous waste* which is hard to get rid of safely. Hazardous waste includes anything that is toxic, or poisonous; anything that can suddenly explode or catch fire; anything that is corrosive, like a strong chemical that might burn a hole in cloth, metal, or a person's skin.

If you throw away a spray can that still has pressure in it, it may explode when crushed in the garbage truck. The spray or cleaner that is left inside the can may also be dangerous.

This sign on San Francisco buses was part of a campaign to alert people to the problem of household hazardous waste.

(City of San Francisco Solid Waste Management Program)

Insecticides, pesticides used to get rid of rats and other pests, and herbicides used to kill weeds can be toxic. The clue is in the four letters, *cide,* at the end of each word. *Cide* means "killer." Arsenic is one of the most famous killers. Writers of murder mysteries often use it to poison their victims. Most people wouldn't think they had such a powerful poison in the house, but arsenic is an ingredient of many pesticides.

One million dead car batteries need to be disposed of each year. Inside each battery are nineteen pounds of lead and a gallon of sulfuric acid. Lead is known to cause brain damage in human beings. A drop of sulfuric acid would burn a hole in your shirt or skin. Both lead and sulfuric acid are hazardous if they get into the air we breathe or the water we drink. Old car batteries should be taken to service stations or recycling centers.

Small batteries for toys, tape players, radios, and watches are also dangerous to throw into the trash because they may contain mercury or cadmium. Mercury, cadmium, chromium, and lead are called *heavy metals.* Even small amounts of most heavy metals are poisonous. A century ago when Lewis Carroll was writing *Alice in Wonderland,* hat makers used mercury in preparing the felt for the fashionable top hats. Breathing in mercury fumes slowly affected their brains, and there was a saying "mad as a hatter," which inspired the Mad Hatter character in *Alice.*

The engines in cars and lawn mowers need motor oil and lubricants to run. From time to time the dirty oil must be drained out and fresh oil put in. Motor oil is deadly to plants and ruins the soil, and it is poisonous when it gets into streams or drinking water. Garbage collectors won't take it. But service stations and recycling centers will; they sell it to companies who clean it and recycle it as fuel oil.

Antifreeze is used in car radiators during the winter. It too needs to be changed from time to time, but it should not be carelessly poured on the street or in the yard. It is toxic

All states encourage recycling motor oil. In Alabama, Project ROSE collects more than eight million gallons of used oil each year.

(Project ROSE, a service mark of the University of Alabama, sponsored by the Science, Technology, and Energy Division of ADECA [Alabama Dept. of Economic and Community Affairs])

and can kill a pet or small child who samples it. Dogs and cats, in particular, seem to be attracted to the taste of antifreeze.

If you've ever taken a whiff of ammonia or bleach, you know they are strong stuff. Handle them with care. Never, never mix them together, as the mixture creates a very poisonous gas. Most household cleaners contain strong chemicals such as ammonia or chlorine, which are useful in killing germs but are poisonous and often corrosive. When they are thrown in with other solid waste, there is a chance they will mix with something that causes them to catch fire or explode.

Silver polish, floor polish, rug cleaners, drain cleaners, photographic chemicals, and swimming-pool chemicals are other products that become hazardous waste. They and their containers should be kept out of the garbage. A safe way to get rid of them is to save them for a "Hazardous Waste Collection Day." Many towns hold these every year. The waste is taken by a hazardous waste company whose

This Hazardous Waste Collection Day in Brevard County, Florida, is one of hundreds sponsored by communities in all parts of the country to help families dispose of toxic products.

(Florida Department of Environmental Regulation)

business it is to separate and handle the chemicals and poisons safely.

When people talk about the problem of hazardous waste, they are usually talking about the careless dumping of large amounts of chemicals and other trash by factories, hospitals, and even stores. For many years, people did not know or pay attention to how harmful industrial trash could be. Then Lois Gibbs at Love Canal, New York, discovered what was causing so much sickness in her neighborhood. Hundreds of gallons of old chemicals had been buried there before the houses were built. Love Canal made everyone aware of the potential danger of hazardous waste sites.

Some years later, people in New York, New Jersey, and Connecticut were horrified to find plastic gloves, syringes, and other illegally dumped medical waste washed up on their beaches during the summer. The beaches were closed and no one could go swimming. The public had been alerted to the importance of disposing of medical waste safely.

Old tires are not hazardous waste, but even so the garbage collectors won't take them, because the landfills won't accept them. The trouble is that tires won't stay put. Try squeezing a tire. The minute you let go, it pops back. When tires are buried, they slowly but surely work their way up to the top of the landfill. Tires will burn, but since the grate of an incinerator's furnace is on a slant, they often roll down and out of the fire before they get hot enough to disintegrate. Tires are hard to recycle because many of them are steel belted, meaning threads of steel run through the rubber. There are at least 240 million tires discarded each year — another solid waste problem waiting to be solved.

Tires dumped ten years ago in an old gravel bank are still there. 240 million tires are discarded each year.

(Joseph S. Coppola)

CHAPTER ELEVEN

THINK ABOUT GARBAGE

Some people say that we have become a throwaway society. What they mean is that Americans throw everything in the garbage without thinking about how much they waste. It would be smarter to buy things that last and to find ways to reuse and recycle materials. These are the three R's of cutting down on solid waste: Reduce, Reuse, and Recycle.

People have always thrown away garbage and trash. Scientists have even found the trash of prehistoric cave dwellers. Archaeologists, the scientists who study ancient peoples, eagerly dig in ancient garbage and trash piles, carefully writing down everything they find. Bones, seeds, cracked pottery, and broken spears all tell us something about what people of long ago ate and how they lived.

William Rathje is an archaeologist at the University of Arizona. Instead of studying ancient trash, he has been studying the garbage of our throwaway society. He and his students look into garbage cans and dig into landfills. They've learned some surprising things.

One thing Rathje has discovered is that many items in our landfills are not biodegrading as fast as people expected them to. He found that in one place he could tell what garbage had been buried every February for years back. At different levels he uncovered thick layers of phone books, buried every February when new phone books are delivered and old ones thrown out. Therefore, he knew the garbage immediately above and below a layer of phone books was probably tossed out in the same month.

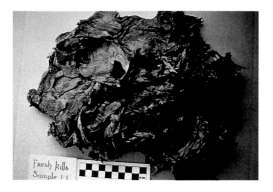

Fresh Kills
Sample 1-1

THE ARIZONA REPU

Phoenix, Arizona, Friday, July 30, 1971

Apollo orbits moon

Scott calls lunar view 'absolutely mind boggling'

Dr. Rathje also found out that most people don't pay much attention to what or how much they throw away. They are happy to have garbage and trash disappear with the garbage truck. For years few people talked about garbage or knew it was becoming a problem.

Then in the spring of 1987, three thousand tons of garbage suddenly became famous. This garbage had no place to go. No one wanted it. It was on a barge pulled by a seagoing tug, named *Break of Dawn*, which sailed from Long Island. The tug's captain was told to deliver the garbage to a landfill in North Carolina. When they got there, North Carolina officials said, "No, take it somewhere else." So they sailed on to Louisiana, then to Florida. No one would let them leave the garbage. They went to the country of Belize in Central America and to the Bahamas. No luck. Mexico and Cuba sent gunboats out to keep the wandering garbage barge away. *Break of Dawn* and the unwanted barge wandered for six months before arrangements were finally made for them to return to New York.

Millions of people followed this journey in the newspapers and on television. Everyone made jokes about the homeless garbage. But the troubles of *Break of Dawn* and its famous load of garbage woke people up, making them think about how much garbage we create and what happens to it.

Lettuce would normally decompose in two to six weeks. This head was buried in a landfill for five years. The newspaper was buried for eighteen years.

(W. Copas, The Garbage Project, Univ. of Arizona)

The amount of solid waste is growing every year, and with it the problem of disposal. How much must be buried? How much should be burned? How much can be composted or recycled? Is it possible for us to change our habits and reduce the amount of garbage and trash? These questions are being hotly debated. There are no easy answers or ready solutions.

Solving our garbage problem will take many years. It will take imagination, new ideas, money, and hard work. Some solutions will come from new laws. Some will come from new inventions. Some will come from people changing what they buy and how they use it.

What will your part be in solving these problems? Will you dream up new ways to reuse things? Will you design a new kind of packaging that uses less material? Will you help people understand the importance of recycling? Will you invent a new way to make use of ash from incinerators? Will you study the science of landfills and make them safer? New ideas and solutions need to be found, and perhaps you'll be among the people who find them.

GLOSSARY

bacteria: One-celled microorganisms.

baghouse: Pollution-control device used in an incinerator.

bale: Material squeezed into a large square bundle to make it easier to transport.

biodegradable: Describes a material that can be broken down by bacteria and natural processes into stable compounds such as carbon dioxide and water.

ceramic: Made of baked clay, such as pottery, china, earthenware, and tiles.

compost: A mixture of decomposing vegetable matter, manure, etc. that can be used to improve the soil.

contaminate: To make impure or infected by adding another substance.

corrosive: Describes a substance that eats into or wears away other material.

crude oil: Petroleum, or oil, as it is pumped from the ground, before it goes to the refinery.

decompose: To break down, come apart, or change form.

disposable: Describes something that is intended to be thrown away after use.

ferrous metals: Those such as steel that are made mainly of iron.

fly ash: Small particles of ash and soot generated by the burning of coal, oil, or solid waste.

garbage: The part of solid waste that is food; also used to mean everything a household throws away and anything that is considered worthless.

hazardous waste: Waste that creates a problem for living creatures or the environment because it is: 1. toxic, 2. corrosive, 3. explosive, or 4. flammable. Waste that carries disease or is radioactive is also classified as hazardous waste.

heavy metals: Those with a specific gravity higher than 5.0, such as lead, mercury, cadmium, and chromium.

incinerator: A building designed to burn solid waste.

ingot: Metal formed into a rectangular shape.

landfill: A place where solid waste is buried.

leachate: Liquid that drains from a landfill and contains potentially harmful material.

materials recycling facility (MRF): A building designed to process recyclable materials collected from homes so that they can be sold to companies that will use them to manufacture something new. It may also be called an intermediate processing center or IPC.

methane: A colorless, odorless, flammable gas (Ch4) present in natural gas and formed by the decomposition of vegetable matter.

microbe: A microorganism. Generally used to refer to bacteria.

microorganism: Any animal or vegetable so small that it can only be seen through a microscope.

molecule: The smallest particle of an element or compound that can exist in a free state and still retain the characteristics of the element or compound.

packaging: A wrapping or container used for one or more of these reasons: 1. to keep the product clean, fresh, or pure; 2. to reduce damage and loss; 3. to make it easier to use; 4. to make it more attractive and easier to sell.

pollute: To put a substance in the air, water, or land that causes dirtiness, impurity, or unhealthiness.

recycle: To collect a waste product and use it in making the same or another product.

recycling center: A collection place for recyclable materials such as glass, metal, paper, and oil.

refinery: A place where metal is extracted from ore or where a raw material such as crude oil is purified.

resource recovery facility: A building where solid waste is used to create some form of energy. Also called a waste-to-energy facility.

reuse: To extend the life of a product by repairing it or creating a new use for it.

sanitary landfill: A specially engineered landfill, constructed so that it reduces hazards to public health and safety.

scrap steel: Metal recovered from discarded products made of steel, which is reused in the steel-making process.

scrubber: Pollution-control device used in an incinerator.

sludge: The solid material that remains when the water is taken out of liquid waste or sewage to be cleaned and purified.

solid waste: Household solid waste, also called residential solid waste, includes garbage, trash, yard waste, and bulky waste such as white goods. A combination of household waste and commercial waste is called municipal waste. Other kinds of solid waste include agricultural, mining, and industrial solid waste.

toxic: Poisonous.

transfer station: A place where solid waste, brought in by small collection trucks, is put into large trucks or barges for transportation to a disposal site.

trash: Everything that is thrown away or considered worthless, with the exception of food.

waste-to-energy facility: A place where municipal solid waste is burned to generate steam or electricity.

white goods: Discarded large appliances such as refrigerators, bathtubs, etc., which are largely made of steel. Years ago such appliances were almost always white in color.

SOME SOURCES FOR MORE INFORMATION

Beame, Rona. *What Happens to Garbage?* Englewood Cliffs, NJ: Julian Messner, 1975. Follows the people who collect and dispose of New York City's solid waste. Contains an interesting chapter on what happens to the debris when buildings are torn down.

Catton, Cris, and James Gray. *The Incredible Heap: A Guide to Compost Gardening.* New York: St. Martin's Press, 1983. Includes history and science as well as how-to information.

Crampton, Norm. *Complete Trash: The Best Way to Get Rid of Practically Everything Around the House.* New York: M. Evans & Co., 1989. Serious information presented with a light touch.

Earthworks Group. *Fifty Simple Things Kids Can Do to Save the Earth.* Kansas City, MO: Andrews and McMeel, 1990. Full of tips and experiments such as how to find out what is biodegradable.

Environmental Action Coalition. *It's Your Environment, Things to Think About, Things to Do.* New York: Charles Scribner's Sons, 1976. The best from *Eco-News,* a wonderful newsletter for young readers.

Freudenthal, Ralph, and Susan Loy. *What You Need to Know to Live with Chemicals.* Green Farms, CT: Hill Publishing, 1989. Written to give non-scientists some understanding of the biology and chemistry of environmental issues.

Garbage, The Practical Journal for the Environment published bimonthly by Old-House Journal Corp. (435 Ninth Street, Brooklyn, NY 11215). A magazine with up-to-date, readable articles filled with interesting information and practical advice on a wide range of subjects.

MacEachern, Diane. *Save Our Planet: 750 Everyday Ways You Can Help Clean Up the Earth.* New York: Dell Publishing Co., 1990. Suggestions for reducing, reusing, and recycling.

Office of Solid Waste. *Solid Waste Dilemma — an Agenda for Action,* Final Report of the Municipal Solid Waste Task Force. Washington, DC: U.S. Environmental Protection Agency, 1989.

Pringle, Laurence. *Throwing Things Away, from Middens to Resource Recovery.* New York: Thomas Y. Crowell Co., 1986. Filled with interesting details about ancient and modern dumps and landfills.

Simons, Robin. *Recyclopedia: Games, Science Equipment, and Crafts from Recycled*

Materials. Boston: Houghton Mifflin Co., 1976. The Recycle Center of the Boston Children's Museum collects scrap material from many sources and makes it available for teachers and others to use in craft projects. How to set up such a center is described in the introduction. The rest of the book gives wonderful ideas on what can be made with scraps and trash.

Washington State Department of Ecology. *A-way with Waste: A Waste Management Curriculum for Schools.* 2nd ed. Redmond, WA: Waste Reduction, Recycling and Litter Control Program, 1989. 352 pages of interesting activities that challenge thinking about all the different facets of our solid waste program.

ORGANIZATIONS

Many environmental organizations are concerned with solid waste programs and solutions. These are a few of them.

Environmental Defense Fund, 257 Park Avenue South, New York, NY 10010.

Institute for Local Self-Reliance, 2425 Eighteenth Street, NW, Washington, DC 20009.

Waste Watch Center, 16 Haverhill Street, Andover, MA 01810.

Various professional and manufacturers' organizations are also concerned about solid waste and recycling. Some of those that will send you information are:

National Solid Waste Management Association, 1730 Rhode Island Avenue, NW, Washington, DC 20036.

Keep America Beautiful, Inc., Mill River Plaza, 9 West Broad Street, Stamford, CT 06902.

Council for Solid Waste Solutions, 1275 K Street NW, Washington, DC 20005.

Steel Can Recycling Institute, Foster Plaza 10, 680 Anderson Drive, Pittsburgh, PA 15220.

Institute of the Scrap Recycling Industries, 1627 K Street, Washington, DC 20006.

Each state government has an environmental agency. This agency will give you information about solid waste management, including recycling, composting, and hazardous waste. Ask for the exact name and address of the agency at your library.

The United States Environmental Protection Agency is the federal agency. It has a Solid Waste Office whose address is 401 M Street, SW, Washington, DC 20460. The EPA also has ten regional offices in different parts of the country. You can get the address of your regional EPA office at your library.

The Marine Debris Information Office of the United States Department of Commerce is at the Center for Marine Conservation, 1725 DeSales Street, NW, Suite 500, Washington, DC 20036.

ACKNOWLEDGMENTS

I am grateful to the many people who have helped and encouraged me in writing this book and gathering the photographs for it. There are those who read the manuscript at its various stages: Kimberly Hedzik and Anita Blumenthal of National Solid Waste Management Association; David P. Sutherland, Connecticut Audubon Society Environmental Center; Orvis Yingling, Nature Center for Environmental Activities; Gloria A. Mills, Ogden Martin Systems, Inc.; Elizabeth Seiler, Keep America Beautiful, Inc.; Beth Topor, James River Corporation; Peggy Winston. Among the many people, organizations, and companies who have helped me in my research are Ryerson Van Deusen; Bristol (CT) Resource Recovery Facility; Bailey L. Condrey, Jr., of Council for Solid Waste Solutions; Dana Duxbury & Associates; Wendell R. Deato of Johnson Controls, Inc.; Tanya Boghossian of Rhode Island Solid Waste Management Corp.; Janet Keller, Division of Environmental Coordination, Rhode Island Dept. of Environmental Management; City of San Francisco's Solid Waste Management Program; Carmen McDougall; Rowland Balleck of Dexter Associates; Ronald Thomas of Reynolds Metals Co.; Robert Koslowski of Cornell University; The Garbage Project, University of Arizona; Janet McCarthy Grimm, Lindenmeyer Nature Center for Environmental Activities.

Special thanks to my editor, Dorothy Briley, for her encouragement; to her assistant editor, Leslie Kriesel; and to my husband, Joseph S. Coppola.

INDEX

air pollution, 11, 14, 17, 22–25, 43
aluminum, 28–32, 36, 38–39, 44–46
ammonia, 17, 52
antifreeze, 51–52
archaeologists, 55–56
arsenic, 51
ash, 22, 23, 25–26

bacteria, 16–19
baghouse, 25
batteries, 8, 24, 50, 51
biodegradable, 18, 20–21, 42, 46
"bottle bill," 31
Break of Dawn (tugboat and garbage barge), 56
bulky waste, 9

Center for Marine Conservation, 34
ceramics, 18, 23, 39–40
chemicals, 24, 25, 49, 50, 52, 53
cleaners, 50, 52
cloth, 6, 27, 28
collection trucks, 8–10, 13–15, 24, 36–37, 50, 56
compost, 19–20, 57
corrosives, 50–52

decomposition, 17–19
disease, 10, 22
disposables, 46. *See also* throwaways

electricity, 23, 25, 30
energy, production or saving of, 17–18, 23–24, 31, 32, 49

environmental concerns, 14, 32, 34, 35, 57
explosion, possibility of, 17, 50, 52

ferrous metals, 38. *See also* iron; steel
fire, 10–11, 12, 17, 23–25, 50, 52
flies, 10, 12
fly ash, 25
food, 6–7, 9, 16–17, 19, 42, 44–47, 56
fungi, 16

garage sales, 28
garbage
    amount of, 6, 8, 11, 44–45, 57
    burning of, 22–26, 43, 57
    burying of, 12–15, 57
    collection of, 8–10
    defined, 9
    dumping of, 10–11, 53–54
    transporation of, 15
gases, 16–18, 23, 25, 41–43, 52
glass, 6, 18, 23, 31, 35, 36, 38–40, 42, 44

hazardous waste, 50–54
Hazardous Waste Collection Day, 52–53
heavy metals, 51
household waste, 6, 9
humus, 19
hydrochloric acid, 25

incinerators, 22–26, 46, 54, 57
industrial waste, 29, 53
insecticides, 50, 51
iron, 26, 32, 38

landfills, 12–18, 19, 20, 22–23, 25–26, 32, 46, 54, 55–57
  amount buried in, 13, 19
  closing of, 14–15, 22
  sanitary, 14–18
laws, 34, 49, 53, 57
leachate, 11, 14
lead, 51
leaves, 19–21
liquid waste, 9
litter, 34, 43, 46
Love Canal, 53

magnets, 26, 38, 39
materials recycling facility (MRF), 36–39
medical waste, 53–54
mercury, 51
metal, 6, 9, 18, 32–33, 35, 38, 42, 51
methane, 17–18
microorganisms, 16–18, 19, 21
mulch, 20

oil, 41, 50–52

packaging, 7–8, 29–34, 38–42, 44–46, 50, 57
paint, 8, 50
paper, 6, 8, 18, 19, 29, 35–37, 42, 44, 45–49
pesticides, 51
plastics, 6–7, 13, 16, 18, 27, 31, 34, 35–36, 38–43, 44–46, 53
polishes, 50, 52
pollution control devices, 25

rags, 35
rate, 10, 12
Rathje, William, 55–56

recycling, 27–33, 35–42, 46–49, 51, 54, 55, 57
recycling center, 35–37, 57
recycling symbols, 29, 40–41, 49
reducing amount of materials used, 46, 49, 55
refineries, 30–32, 41
refuse, 9
resource recovery facility, 23–26
reusing materials, 27–29, 35, 53, 57

sanitary landfills. *See* landfills
sanitation workers, 9, 12
scrubbers, 25
sewage, 9, 20
sludge, 20
smoke, 11, 23
solid waste, 9. *See also* garbage
spray cans, 7, 50
steel, 26, 28, 29, 32, 36, 38
sulfuric acid, 51

throwaways, 44–46, 49, 55
tin, 32
tires, 28, 54
town dump, 10, 22
toxic substances, 11, 14, 43, 50–53
transfer station, 15
trash, 9, 27–29, 34. *See also* garbage

waste-to-energy facility, 23. *See also* resource recovery facility
water pollution, 11, 13, 14, 34
white goods, 9, 32, 33
wood, 6, 18, 19–20, 28, 42, 47, 48, 49

yard waste, 6, 19